MOODY MARGARET
Casts a Spell

MOODY MARGARET
Casts a Spell

Francesca Simon
Illustrated by Tony Ross

Orion
Children's Books

Moody Margaret Cast a Spell originally appeared in
Horrid Henry Meets the Queen first published in
Great Britain in 2004 by Orion Children's Books
This edition first published in Great Britain in 2012
by Orion Children's Books
a division of the Orion Publishing Group Ltd
Orion House
5 Upper Saint Martin's Lane
London WC2H 9EA
An Hachette UK Company

1 3 5 7 9 10 8 6 4 2

A catalogue record for this book is available from the British Library.

ISBN 978 1 4440 0117 4
Printed in China

www.orionbooks.co.uk
www.horridhenry.co.uk

To the Three Musketeers:
Hannah; Noah and Eve.
With love from Sarah and Alan

Look out for . . .

Don't Be Horrid, Henry!
Horrid Henry's Birthday Party
Horrid Henry's Holiday
Horrid Henry's Underpants
Horrid Henry Gets Rich Quick
Horrid Henry and the Football Fiend
Horrid Henry's Nits
Horrid Henry and Moody Margaret
Horrid Henry's Thank You Letter
Horrid Henry Reads A Book
Horrid Henry's Car Journey
Moody Margaret's School
Horrid Henry Tricks and Treats
Horrid Henry's Christmas Play
Horrid Henry's Rainy Day
Horrid Henry's Author Visit
Horrid Henry Meets the Queen
Horrid Henry's Sports Day

There are many more **Horrid Henry** books
available. For a complete list visit
www.horridhenry.co.uk
or
www.orionbooks.co.uk

Contents

Chapter 1

"You are getting sleepy,"
said Moody Margaret.
"You are getting very sleepy . . ."
Slowly she waved her watch
in front of Susan.

"So sleepy . . . you are now asleep
. . . you are now fast asleep . . ."

"No I'm not," said Sour Susan.

"When I click my fingers
you will start snoring."
Margaret clicked her fingers.

"But I'm not asleep," said Susan.

Margaret glared at her.
"How am I supposed
to hypnotise you
if you don't try?"
said Margaret.

"I am trying,
you're just a bad
hypnotist," said
Susan sourly.
"Now it's my
turn."

"No it's not, it's still mine,"
said Margaret.

"You've had your go," said Susan.

"No I haven't!"

"But I never get to be the
hypnotist!" wailed Susan.

"Cry baby!"

"Meanie!"

"Cheater!"

"Cheater!"

Slap!

Slap!

Susan glared at Margaret.
Why was she friends with such
a mean moody bossyboots?

Margaret glared at Susan.
Why was she friends with such
a stupid sour sulker?

"I hate you, Margaret!"
screamed Sour Susan.

"I hate you more!"
screamed Moody Margaret.

Chapter 2

"Shut up, landlubbers!" shrieked
Horrid Henry from his hammock
in the garden next door.
"Or the Purple Hand will make you
walk the plank!"

"Shut up yourself, Henry,"
said Margaret.

"Yeah, Henry," said Susan.

"You are stupid, you are stupid,"
chanted Rude Ralph, who was
playing pirates with Henry.

"You're the stupids,"
snapped Moody Margaret.
"Now leave us alone, we're busy."

"Henry, can I play pirates with you?"
asked Perfect Peter, wandering out
from the house.

"No, you puny prawn!"
screamed Captain Hook.
"Out of my way before I tear you
to pieces with my hook!"

"Muuum," wailed Peter.
"Henry said he was going to
tear me to pieces!"

"Stop being horrid, Henry!"
shouted Mum.

"And he won't let me play
with him," said Peter.

"Can't you be nice to your brother
for once?" said Dad.

NO! thought Horrid Henry.
Why should he be nice to that
tell-tale brat?

Horrid Henry did not want
to play pirates with Peter.

Peter was the world's **worst** pirate.

He couldn't swordfight.

He couldn't swashbuckle.

He couldn't remember pirate curses.

All he could do was whine.

"Okay, Peter, you're the prisoner. Wait in the fort," said Henry.

"But I'm always the prisoner," said Peter.

"Do you want to play or don't you?"

"Yes, Captain," said Peter.
He crawled into the lair of the
Purple Hand.

Being prisoner was better than nothing, he supposed. He just hoped he wouldn't have to wait too long.

Chapter 3

"Let's get out of here quick,"
Henry whispered to Rude Ralph.
"I've got a great idea for playing a
trick on Margaret and Susan."

He whispered to Ralph.
Ralph grinned.

Horrid Henry hoisted himself onto
the low brick wall between his
garden and Margaret's.
Moody Margaret was still waving
her watch at Susan.

Unfortunately, Susan had her back
turned and her arms folded.

"Go away, Henry,"
ordered Margaret.

"Yeah, Henry," said Susan.
"No boys."

"Are you being hypnotists?"
said Henry.

"Margaret's trying to hypnotise me,
only she can't 'cause she's a rubbish
hypnotist," said Susan.

"That's your fault,"
said Margaret, glaring.

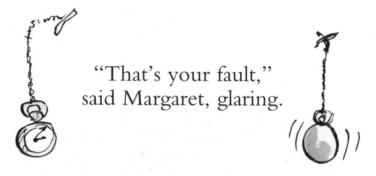

"Of course you can't hypnotise her,"
said Henry.
"You're doing it all wrong."

"And what would you know about that?" asked Margaret.

"Because," said Horrid Henry, "I am a master hypnotist."

Moody Margaret laughed.
"He is too a master hypnotist,"
said Ralph.
"He hypnotises me all the time."

"Oh yeah?" said Margaret.

"Yeah," said Henry.

"Prove it," said Margaret.

"Okay," said Henry.
"Gimme the watch."

Margaret handed it over.

He turned to Ralph.
"Look into my eyes," he ordered.

Ralph looked into Henry's eyes.

"Now watch the watch,"
ordered Henry the hypnotist,
swinging the watch back and forth.

Rude Ralph swayed.

"You will obey my commands,"
said Henry.

"I – will – obey," said Ralph
in a robot voice.

"When I whistle, you will jump
off the wall," said Henry.
He whistled.

Ralph jumped off the wall.

"See?" said Horrid Henry.

Chapter 4

"That doesn't prove he's hypnotised," said Margaret. "You have to make him do silly things."

"Like what?" said Henry.

"Tell him he's got no clothes on."

"Ralph, you're a nudie," said Henry.

Ralph immediately started running
round the garden shrieking.
"Aaaaaaarrgghh!" yelped Ralph.
"I'm a nudie! I'm a nudie!
Give me some clothes, help, help!
No one look, I'm naked!"

Margaret hesitated. There was no way Henry could have really hypnotised Ralph – was there?

"I still don't believe he's hypnotised," said Margaret.

"Then watch this,"
said Horrid Henry.
"Ralph – when I snap my fingers
you will be … Margaret."

Snap!

"My name is Margaret," said Ralph.
"I'm a mean bossyboots.
I'm the biggest bossiest boot.
I'm a frogface."

Margaret blushed red.
Susan giggled.
"It's not funny," snapped Margaret.
No one made fun of her and
lived to tell the tale.

"See?" said Henry.
"He obeys my every command."

"**Wow**,"
said Susan.
"You really
are a hypnotist.
Can you teach me?"

"Maybe," said
Horrid Henry.
"How much will
you pay me?"

"He's just a big faker," said Margaret.
She stuck her nose in the air.
"If you're such a great hypnotist,
then hypnotise *me*."

Oops.

Now he was trapped.
Margaret was trying to spoil his trick.
Well, no way would he let her.

Chapter 5

Horrid Henry remembered
who he was.

The boy who got
Miss Battle-Axe
sent to the head.

The boy who
terrified the
bogey babysitter

The boy who
tricked the
Tooth Fairy.

He could hypnotise Margaret any
day. "Sure," he said, waving the
watch in front of Margaret.
"You are getting sleepy,"
droned Henry.

"You are getting very sleepy.
When I snap my fingers you will
obey my every command."
Henry snapped his fingers.

Margaret glared at him.

"Well?" said Moody Margaret.

"Don't you know *anything*?" said
Horrid Henry. He thought fast.
"That was just the beginning bit.
I will complete Part Two once
I have freed Ralph from my power.
Ralph, repeat after me,
'I am sellotape'."

"I am sellotape," said Rude Ralph.
Then he belched.

"I am burping sellotape," said
Rude Ralph. He caught Henry's eye.
They burst out laughing.
"Ha ha, Susan, fooled you!"
shrieked Henry.

"Did not," shrieked Susan.

"Did too. Nah nah ne nah nah!"
Henry and Ralph ran round
Margaret, whooping and cheering.

"Come on, Margaret," said Susan. "Let's do some *real* hypnosis." Margaret didn't move.

"Come on, Margaret," said Susan.

"I am sellotape," said Margaret.

"No you're not," said Susan.

"Yes I am," said Margaret.

Henry and Ralph stopped whooping.

"There's something wrong with
Margaret," said Susan.
"She's acting all funny.
Margaret, are you okay?
Margaret? Margaret?"

Chapter 6

Moody Margaret stood very still.
Her eyes looked blank.

Henry snapped his fingers.
"Raise your right arm," he ordered.
Margaret raised her right arm.

Huh? thought Horrid Henry.

"Pinch Susan."
Margaret pinched Susan.

"Owwww!" yelled Susan.

"Repeat after me,
'I am a stupid girl'."

"I am a stupid girl," said Margaret.

"No you're not," said Susan.

"Yes I am," said Margaret.

"She's hypnotised,"
said Horrid Henry.
He'd actually hypnotised
Moody Margaret. This was amazing.
This was fantastic. He really truly
was a master hypnotist!

"Will you obey me, slave?"

"I will obey," said Margaret.

"When I click my fingers, you will
be a ... chicken."

Click!

"Squawk! Squawk! Squawk!" cackled Margaret, flapping her arms wildly.

"What have you done to her?" wailed Sour Susan.

"Wow," said Rude Ralph. "You've hypnotised her."

Horrid Henry could not
believe his luck.

If he could hypnotise Margaret,
he could hypnotise anyone.

Everyone would have to obey
his commands. He would be master
of the world! The universe!
Everything!

Henry could see it now.
"Henry, ten out of ten,"
Miss Battle-Axe would say.
"Henry is so clever he doesn't ever
need to do homework again."

Oh boy, would he fix
Miss Battle-Axe.

He'd make her do the hula in a grass
skirt when she wasn't running round
the playground mooing like a cow.

He'd make the head Mrs Oddbod
just have chocolate and cake for
school dinners.

And no P.E. – ever.
In fact, he'd make Mrs Oddbod
close down the school.

And as for Mum and Dad . . .

"Henry, have as many sweets as you like," Dad would say.

"No bedtime for you,"
Mum would say.

"Henry, watch as much TV as you
want," Dad would say.

"Henry, here's your pocket money –
£1000 a week. Tell us if you need
more," Mum would smile.

"Peter, go to your room and stay
there for a year!" Mum and Dad
would scream.

Henry would hypnotise them
all later. But first, what should he
make Margaret do?
Ah yes. Her house was filled with
sweets and biscuits and fizzy drinks —
all the things Henry's horrible parents
never let him have.

"Bring us all your sweets, all your biscuits and a Fizzywizz drink."

"Yes, master," said Moody Margaret.

Chapter 7

Henry stretched out in the
hammock. So did Rude Ralph.
This was the life!

Sour Susan didn't know what to do. On the one hand, Margaret was mean and horrible, and she hated her. It was fun watching her obey orders for once. On the other hand, Susan would much rather Margaret was *her* slave than Henry's.

"Unhypnotise her, Henry,"
said Sour Susan.

"Soon," said Horrid Henry.

"Let's hypnotise Peter next,"
said Ralph.

"Yeah," said Henry. No more
telling tales. No more goody goody
vegetable-eating I'm Mr Perfect.
Oh boy would he hypnotise Peter!

Moody Margaret came slowly out
of her house. She was carrying a
large pitcher and a huge bowl of
chocolate mousse.

"Here is your Fizzywizz drink,
master," said Margaret.
Then she poured it on top of him.

"Wha . . . ? Wha . . . ?" spluttered
Henry, gasping and choking.

"And your dinner, frogface,"
she added, tipping the mousse
all over Ralph.

"Ugggh!" wailed Ralph.

"Nah Nah Ne Nah Nah,"
shrieked Margaret.
"Fooled you! Fooled you!"

Perfect Peter crept out of the
Purple Hand Fort. What was all that
yelling? It must be a pirate mutiny!

"Hang on, pirates, here I come!"
shrieked Peter, charging at the
thrashing hammock as fast
as he could.

CRASH!

A sopping wet pirate captain
and a mousse-covered first mate lay
on the ground. They stared up at
their prisoner.

"Hi, Henry," said Peter.
"I mean, hi, Captain."
He took a step backwards. "I mean,
Lord High Excellent Majesty."
He took another step back.
"Ugh, we were playing pirate
mutiny, weren't we?"

"Die, Worm!"
yelled Horrid Henry, leaping up.

"Muuuuuum!" shrieked Peter.